The Thing I Was Trying to Tell You

The Thing I Was Trying to Tell You

Joseph Young

Publishing Genius Press
Westport, NY

CONTENTS

The Thing I Was Trying to Tell You // 1

Peter and the Fish // 3

Tall Grass // 5

Like Dark // 7

The Drop // 8

Mirror of Chance // 10

The Most Exciting Things // 11

One Last Presser for the Caballero of Berlin // 13

Aha Again // 15

Ms. Z— // 17

Heart Shaped Box // 19

Nevertheless // 21

Ars longa, vita brevis // 22

The Sorrow // 33

1974 // 35

Black Crow and Snow // 37

Mystery and Manners // 40

The Council // 43

Eleven Things My Mother Told Me // 45

Science from Stephen Jay Gould // 46

Pledge // 47

The Pants // 49

41 School Girls: A Play // 50

Greasy White and Blue Kittens // 53

Objects I Keep Abusing // 56

Your Mother the Minimalist // 57

Fauna of My Front Yard // 58

The Platypus // 67

Everything is interesting, everything is good // 69

Red in Tooth // 71

The Murder // 73

The Paintings of Forrest Bess // 75

Cambrian Explosion // 78

Politics // 80

The Wall // 82

New Metaphors in Flash Fiction // 84

Of All the Creatures These Are the Creatures
   That Talk the Most // 86

Nervous-Ghosts; or, The Utilities of Wonder // 89

Blue Ridge // 92

Ecological study of a bat colony in the tropical
   rain forest of Peru // 94

Art Cop // 95

June Cobb // 97

The Spanish Acre // 100

Applause Please // 101

Markus Rothkowitz—All Over // 104

A New Practical Treatise on the Three Primitive
    Colours Assumed as a Perfect System of
    Rudimentary Information // 106

Something About Easter, Maybe // 108

Is the **Black Place** Gray? // 110

A Pair of Men // 112

You Must Change Your Life // 114

Princess Cecilie Viktoria Anastasia Zeta Thyra
    Adelheid of Prussia // 116

Orientation // 118

Law // 121

Work // 122

Basho : Champ of Haiku : Comes for Late
    Summertime Lunch // 123

Birds // 125

Watching Paint Dry // 127

Barbie Football // 129

The Artist (a fiction) // 132

The Return // 134

Plato's Old Blind Elephant // 136

How to Write Flash Fiction // 139

About the Author // 149

Acknowledgments // 150

The Thing I Was Trying to Tell You

Take any three things, she said, beginning to draw a triangle in the air. One: a man lying alone in a field. Two: a dog hit by a car....

She went still for a moment, the third side of her shape undone.

Yes? he answered.

I don't know, she said. A bicycle dropped from a rooftop?

Okay, he said. Those three things.

Okay. She stuck a finger in the corner of her eye. Take any of those three things and consider them. Then, think of them as seen by a child, a small girl or boy.

Oh, he said, okay. How small? he asked. Five? He put out five fingers.

She shook her head, her gold earrings waving. No—not five. Three.

Hmm, he said. *Really* small then.

Yes. Very young. So young, they're hardly even lingual yet.

The clock swung its hand around, a black arc on the kitchen wall. The winter's day drew very little light.

So, he said. Think of that little girl or boy, seeing one of those things?

She nodded. Right. Can you? She peered at him closely. Can you imagine that? Can you see that small child seeing one of those things?

I think so, he said. Probably?

Try, she said. Try very hard. In that way, you'll see what I've been trying to tell you.

Peter and the Fish

Peter'd been at the river four days. A horse swam by. A burning tree. Three tiny white birds. Though he'd not seen God even once.

A thing you'd say is that he missed TV. The way it leveled all things and went quiet in the brain.

God knew he was there. As He sat on His bank and fished, He'd seen Peter boiling water over a circle of stones. God knew it was safer to stay unseen. The man was practiced in the pitching of sticks.

Peter was all but ready to run out of steam. Over the month he'd been sick: four times. His eyes and lungs were heavy with foam. His mouth was never not dry. If God didn't come soon, Peter'd go back to his city.

He missed his child. The boy he called John who'd been born as Sam, who his wife called Ted.

God wore a faded hat with trout flies tied to the brim. He had a mesh vest with 17 pockets. His jeans were lined with red flannel.

Peter peered into a puddle of rain. God? he said. Are you there? The puddle was silent, though it reflected an avid sun.

John, called Ted, named Sam, owned a green bike. His wife'd built it from a kit. Between the two, who loved Peter more?

Which'd Peter'd loved more: God, wife, or son? Over the year he'd been sick: 12 times. This river and the chance to choose.

He saw a white horse. Three very small birds. A tree like the burning of Rome.

God'd approached from the trees. He held a string of caught fish. Peter? He said, ready to turn on His waders and run.

TALL GRASS

He liked all the cool bands—Sephio, Animal Cache, Tariq Atell—though he didn't like to think of himself that way. Just a music nerd, he'd say, and his friends would agree, roll their eyes, or shrug as was their predisposition.

He was predisposed to Cheerios. Loved them, any time of day.

His girlfriend Betty was about to enter grad school. Oh was she sarcastic! She made the kinds of jokes that made people uncomfortable. She wanted to work with terminally ill children.

Betty and Dylan were engaged. They were both the type to have eschewed the idea of marriage when they were young. Things change. Love.

Dylan was excited to have tickets for the show. Betty always said that upcoming shows made her boyfriend horny. This was true.

Just after they got married Dylan lost his job. He spent six months unemployed. He argued with Betty more than usual—but it was okay. In fact they remained together until Betty got breast cancer, 7 years later.

I love you, she said, but there's just certain things. She moved to, and then died in, Argentina.

Dylan became a music engineer. He got to work with a few of his favorite bands. He was especially fond of musicians just starting out.

Seven years after Betty left him Dylan got remarried. She was nothing like Betty. Well, in some ways she was. Love.

After 7 years Dylan took a trip to Argentina. The beauty took the breath from him. The tall grass kept opening toward the mountains.

Like Dark

Sometimes you have so little to say, she says.

I point at my mouth and shrug.

You think that's cute? she answers.

I lie on my back and waggle my limbs like a baby.

You're an impossible asshole.

This one is tough. All I can think of is to sit perfectly still and imagine the edge of the universe flaking off like pie crust, hope she can see the mystery of it in my eyes.

She gets up and leaves, slamming the iron gate in front of our apartment. She isn't mad though, this is just to keep us from getting bored. She'll go down to the docks and watch the sea lions swim, then come back, smelling like creosote.

Where'd you go? I'll ask, and she'll shake out her caliginous hair.

We were in bed, eating frozen pizza. Carrie had her fingers in her scalp, running auburn strands between her nails, convinced for two weeks straight she had lice. You'll be smelling of pepperoni, I teased her, to which she let out a lowing brook of complaint.

We were watching Agent Cooper walk down one hallway, enter a room of zigzag flooring and leatherette divans, leave it to walk down another. He'd been doing this for a very long time.

For a shorter but very long time, Carrie had been having thoughts of home, the icy springs, pine trees, and manatees of Tallahassee. There are trees there that never touch the ground, she would say, to which no one knew the sense.

I worked in the rigging of the theater myself. Curtains were my métier.

Carrie pressed pause and in the quiet interstice she looked at my hands and the knees beneath them. The young boys in her care were at this time of night at home and asleep.

Robert, she said, and only that. With only that, all our years left the room. There was no time at all—we dropped through a spaceless blanket of stars.

Oh, I said, broken hearted. But I have an idea, I said. An idea.

There was a brightening at the corners of her eyes, for a moment.

Yes? she said. I had one moment, to fix.

The rain was falling on the windows. The moon up there was turning. I never see you, I said, but for a very long time.

What's that? she answered, the gentlest inversion of her chin. Whatever does it mean?

I never see you, I repeated, but for a very long time.

There is something quick to all riddles. You have seen how the most compact of persons will stop, mid-stir, mid-labor, mid-stride.

Carrie kept me fixed for a hundred years. She was a break in the dawn. I'm rising, she replied, doing nothing all at once.

They were kissing in the sand when a wave ran up the beach. Before his lips left hers, they were floating in a 3 foot column of cold water.

The wave receded and dragged them, their yellow lab, and their picnic out to sea. While he rose to the top, she sank, fading among the silt and strands of kelp.

He broke water, sputtering, in time to see his dog and a sea lion regard each other from the crests of parallel swells. The lab, and then the sea lion, began to bark.

He between them—frightened, lungs filled with water, wife nowhere to be seen—became referee in the mirror of chance.

THE MOST EXCITING THINGS

The Bee Gees were weird people. Seriously weird. What was going on in that family? Weird.

I have to go to work today. I haven't been to work in 6 months. This foot. I'm afraid, actually afraid.

The dog's really messed up the back door. Can't anyone just let him out when he wants to go out?

When my grandma bought salami she'd wrap it, double wrap it, put a rubber band around, and then put it in a Tupperware. Nitrates, Grandma, I'd say, but it didn't help.

Sometimes the lake will literally come out of its bowl and march toward the house. Sometimes there's literally fish looking in the sliding door.

They were like, red or white. I was like, white, red stains my teeth. They were like, shrug.

What's better, electric pencil sharpeners or the manual ones? Manual ones go round and round—hurray!

If you've never been to this workshop, it's the best workshop. Are you serious? I say. You never have fucking been???

Go ahead and watch the documentary and tell me they weren't weird. I'll punch you in the mouth.

Things are better now, now that things are better. That's just simple logic, and here comes the coming rain.

One Last Presser for the Caballero of Berlin

Once, he said, when I was on peyote—he waved his palm in front of his face, spread-fingered, in the German sign for crazy—I watched a boy dog birth puppies.

He put his feet out the window, cowboy boots dangling over Manhattan. From below, unseen by anyone else, an 11-year-old tourist looked upwards and laughed.

This was years before, he continued, I'd come to this city, or come anywhere at all. Before I was, how you say, he said—in a Teutonic version of the French pidgin—le movie star.

He was handsome in the way that only requires charisma. Mathilde said later, His teeth were awkward in his mouth and none of us could look away.

Ah well, he said, throwing out his arms—an eerie impression of an elder Lon Chaney—at this point, even the flies are more interesting. Indeed, at the center of the room the flies had made themselves into a quantum-shaped cloud.

I had almost everything I needed, at this point. Edgar had stopped recording. Mathilde sat with her dress about her knees, camera still.

One more question, I said. Who was your favorite?

He turned to me, his lamplight-shadow one beat behind. All of them. I favored them all. All, he said, in a cowpoke Ashkenazi drawl—his flower-worked boots trembling over the long, sad city—my one thousand sisters and ten thousand lovers.

Aha Again

My dad is angry. I should say: again. He's talking about Pharaoh Aha.

Aha, my dad says, he was the guy who did it, you see? My dad is sitting at the head of the table, looking through the window at the yard. The oak trees are turning color and tossing their leaves at the ground.

He was the one to unify Egypt, he says. He took all those little...*principalities*? Yes. He took all those principalities... My dad pauses to glare at us, my sister and I, dares us to challenge the term. ...And he fashions a kingdom.

The housekeeper Charli is upstairs vacuuming. There's the low thunder of its wheels on the rug, the offhand collisions with the furniture. The windowpane through which my dad is viewing the yard shimmers with the efforts of Charli.

But, my dad says, and here he's getting going, they—some of them—claim it was Aha's father. His father! he shouts. The underside of my dad's jaw is turning blue: He's really getting going. His fucking father!

Across the lawn the swans look to hover. They sit their placid way upon the water and the water is the color of the daylight moon. The swans look to hover on the surface of the moon.

My sister laughs. She is the golden child. Aha! she shouts, and it bounces about our paneled room. It was your dad, Aha!

My dad's heart contracts, hidden in his ribs. He is angry. His father. His father's father. He looks at me and divines a dynasty of anger. Charli is shouting at the cat. Charli is running through the hall after the cat. My dad looks at my sister and sees the royal Serekh of love.

I'm in like 45 different text groups. It's the same 8 people but with like one person missing in each one.

Last night we robbed the 7-11. Everyone except Rob. He missed it bc wrong text group.

We didn't really rob it tho. Kevin Slurpee works there on Thursday so we just took every fucking hotdog and emptied out the chili n cheese dispenser. Kevin Slurpee is Rob Slurpee's brother, no cap.

It's like, we're not supposed to be interested in sex anymore. Who came up with that? Okay boomer.

Last night I had sex with Ace. Ace supposedly accordingly doesn't like sex but we did. We were both on our own Porn Hub.

My brother said they're trying to put advertising in space. They'll put ads for Kate Bush in the night sky. If that happens I'll have to be a terrorist.

I'm really in love with Zendaya. Not her actual name but pretty much the same hair same complexion. God I love her. God I love her. God I love her.

Mom loves me. She'll put her hands right in the trash and lift me up. I'll be in the dirt and she'll lift me right the fuck up. I love her and Zendaya and Ace and Rob.

I'll be a terrorist for them if I have to. I'll be a terrorist for anyone who comes after them and for anyone who puts that shit in space and for anyone who shoots a wolf. That's who I am. You shoot a wolf and I'm coming the fuck for you.

HEART SHAPED BOX

He wears a filthy leather apron, leather pants. There's a leather vest and a shirt in the shades of leather. Chest, arms, neck, and face are all of the same color, the color of leather.

As far as you can tell, he's sane. Marxism, he says, it doesn't work.

Is that a joke? you reply.

No, man. His beard the color of leather opens at the mouth in a grin. In fact, he adds, history has just begun. He waves his hand at the street, the cars, the people shopping for records and ducking into hookah bars. It's dialectable, man. Delicious materialisms.

You move on down the street, because whatever he's saying goes over your head. He's frightening, but the odd thing is he doesn't smell. He smells like marigolds.

The kid who's clearly not sane is asking for change in front of the supermarket. His face keeps contorting at the corners.

Why doesn't the leather guy take a bath? you ask him.

The kid stops wobbling and gets reverent in the face. What's that thing in Buddhism?

Life is suffering?

No, bro. The saints. The ones that refuse to go to heaven.

The kid starts melting down in front of you then. His eyes roll back and he's covered in sweat. He's on the ground and someone is calling for Narcan.

You move on down the street. There's the pizza and burrito joint, sex shop and the Zipcar stand. The saint has relocated to the park, under the fig tree in the fog, and he's talking to a woman who's got Nirvana on her iPhone.

This tree is so eminent, says the saint. So immanent. So August. When she doesn't laugh, he points up at the yellow, cardioid leaves.

When she still doesn't laugh, he waves his hand in her face. Are you free? he says, the milky breeze, his animal grin. Have you been blown out?

Under the arc of time a man stands watching. The green river passes, as seen in the ripples of the surfacing pike. His daughter is taking a picture of a willow tree with her grandfather's camera. She finds it funny to crank the lever between photos, to imagine a thing such as film. Her mother, his wife, stands over a puddle, sees the tadpoles swim. Under the arc of time the man checks his phone. His father is in the hospital and his sister texts. His sister is saying, *It's time*. The man steps out from under the arc of time. The path of the sun is just a shape. The breeze is just a breath in the world. *What year am I?* says the man, gripping his head. His daughter turns to him, her mother too. They hold out their hands and say to him, *Dad?*

ARS LONGA, VITA BREVIS

An actor known as Mr. Cummins died on stage while playing the part of Dumont in The Tragedy of Jane Shore by Nicholas Rowe, at the Leeds Theatre in Hunslet. He died of 'ossification of the heart' (aortic stenosis) on 20 June.

Frederick Federici had a heart attack as he descended through a trap door just after singing his last note as Mephistopheles in Gounod's opera Faust at the Princess Theatre in Melbourne.

Alexander Woollcott suffered a heart attack during a Writers' War Board panel on CBS Radio in which he and four other individuals were having a discussion about Hitler.

Albert Stoessel was conducting an orchestra for the American Academy of Arts and Letters in New York, when he died of a heart attack.

Actress Isabel Bonner suffered a heart attack while on stage at the Carthay Circle Theatre in Los Angeles, during a performance of *The Shrike*.

Gareth Jones was portraying a character who died of a heart attack in a live science fiction play Underground in ABC Television's Armchair Theatre television series (30 November) when he died of a real heart attack between his scenes.

Tyrone Power was stricken by a massive heart attack while filming a dueling scene with his frequent co-star and friend, George Sanders for the film Solomon and Sheba.

Actor Louis Jean Heydt died of a heart attack upon conclusion of the first act of the Boston production of There Was a Little Girl, also featuring Jane Fonda.

Singer Leonard Warren expired after performing his aria in the second act of the opera La forza del destino at the New York Metropolitan Opera. He was then to perform Don Carlo's act III aria, which begins Morir, tremenda cosa ("to die, a momentous thing"), when he started coughing and gasping. He fell face first to the ground, and it was revealed he had died of a massive heart attack.

Composer Joseph E. Howard, best known for co-writing "Hello! Ma Baby" and "I Wonder Who's Kissing Her Now," died onstage at Chicago Opera House on 19 May. He collapsed with a heart attack while taking a curtain call after having led the audience in a singalong of the song "Let Me Call You Sweetheart."

Wagnerian bass-baritone Hermann Uhde died on stage of a heart attack during a performance in Copenhagen's Royal Danish Theatre on 10 October.

Professional wrestler Mike DiBiase suffered a heart attack in the ring while wrestling his opponent Man Mountain Mike on 2 July in Lubbock, Texas.

Country music star Spade Cooley died from a heart attack while backstage during the intermission of a benefit concert in Oakland, California on 23 November.

Performer Kenneth Horne, star of the radio comedy show Round the Horne, died of a heart attack while hosting the annual Guild of Television Producers' and Directors' Awards at the Dorchester Hotel in London, moments after the show scriptwriters had received an award and Horne had urged the audience to tune into its next series which had been due to commence shortly.

Actor George Ostroska collapsed from a heart attack at the start of the second act while playing the title role of Macbeth at the Crawford Livingston Theater in St. Paul, Minnesota.

Longevity expert Jerome Rodale was a guest on The Dick Cavett Show. After his interview was done, Pete Hamill was being interviewed by Cavett when Rodale slumped. Hamill, noticing something was wrong, said in a low voice to Cavett, "This looks bad." Rodale had died of a heart attack at age 72.

Luther Lindsay, one of the first black stars in professional wrestling, died of a heart attack at the end of a match.

Godfrey Cambridge, an American comedian, died of a heart attack on the set of Victory at Entebbe at Burbank, California, United States.

Actor Zero Mostel collapsed and died from an aortic aneurysm during the first preview performance of The Merchant, a Broadway-bound adaptation of The Merchant of Venice.

Cuban singer Miguelito Valdés (Mr Babalú) suffered a fatal heart attack while singing at Hotel Tequendama, Bogotá, Colombia, 8 November.

Danish actor and comedian Dirch Passer suffered a fatal heart attack backstage immediately prior to going on stage in Tivoli Gardens on 3 September.

East German comedian Rolf Herricht on 23 August died of a heart attack while acting at Metropol Theater in East Berlin.

Actor and comedian Joe E. Ross suffered a heart attack and died while performing on stage on the evening of 13 August.

Magician and comedian Tommy Cooper suffered a heart attack during a performance on the London Weekend Television variety show Live From Her Majesty's.

Singer Onie Wheeler died of a massive heart attack while performing on the stage of the Grand Ole Opry.

British actor-comedian Leonard Rossiter died of a heart attack in his dressing room at the Lyric Theatre, London whilst preparing to go on stage during a performance in Joe Orton's play Loot.

Actor Adolph Caesar died of a heart attack on the set of the film Tough Guys.

Actress Edith Webster died onstage from a heart attack while performing her death scene in the play "The Drunkard," in a lodge in Baltimore.

Comedian Dick Shawn died on stage while performing at the University of California, San Diego after suffering a fatal heart attack.

British wrestler Mal "King Kong" Kirk died of a pre-existing heart condition after his opponent Big Daddy jumped and landed on him during a match at the Great Yarmouth Hippodrome.

Actor Redd Foxx suffered a fatal heart attack on the set of the CBS sitcom The Royal Family.

Don "Maddog" Wright, jazz clarinetist, died of a heart attack while performing with Greg Brown at The Folkway, a club in Peterborough, New Hampshire.

Polish actor Tadeusz Łomnicki died of a heart attack during one of the last dress rehearsals of Shakespeare's King Lear, in which he was playing the lead role, much awaited by public and critics.

Indian film actor Alummoodan died of a heart attack while performing at the sets of Adwaitham.

Jazz/cabaret singer Sylvia Syms died of a heart attack during a set at New York City's Oak Room at the Algonquin Hotel.

Professional wrestler Larry Cameron died of a heart attack while wrestling a match with Tony St. Clair in Bremen, Germany.

Italian actor Gian Maria Volonté died from a heart attack at the age of 61 at Florina, Greece, during the filming of Ulysses' Gaze.

Beat Farmers singer/drummer/guitarist Country Dick Montana suffered a massive heart attack and died three songs into the band's set at the Long Horn in Whistler, British Columbia, Canada.

Singer Tiny Tim suffered a fatal heart attack while turning to leave the stage during a benefit concert in Minneapolis.

Opera singer Richard Versalle died on stage at the Metropolitan Opera during the company's première performance of The Makropulos Case when he suffered a heart attack while standing on a sliding ladder attached to a file cabinet.

Guitarist/singer Johnny "Guitar" Watson collapsed and died onstage during a performance in Yokohoma, Japan. The cause of death was a heart attack.

Dutchman Coen van Vrijberghe de Coningh died of cardiac arrest during a performance of the television series Flodder.

English reggae performer Judge Dread died from a heart attack as he walked off stage after performing at The Penny Theatre in Canterbury.

Mark Sandman, bassist and lead vocalist for the band Morphine, collapsed on stage at the Giardini del Principe in Palestrina, Latium, Italy (near Rome) while performing with Morphine. He was pronounced dead of a heart attack.

Conductor Giuseppe Sinopoli died of a heart attack while conducting Giuseppe Verdi's Aida at the Deutsche Opera in Berlin.

New Vagrants drummer Joe Forgione died of a heart attack onstage at the Downtime Club, New York.

Scottish actor Gordon Reid collapsed and died on stage from a heart attack at the Finborough Theatre, London, halfway through Act Two of a performance of Samuel Beckett's Waiting for Godot.

Franco Scoglio, Italian football manager and sport TV commenter, died of a heart attack while on the air during a program on the Genoan private TV station Primocanale, after a heated discussion over the phone with Genoa chairman Enrico Preziosi.

Classical pianist and multi-award winner Anthony Burger had a massive heart attack while performing a piano piece entitled "Hear My Song Lord" during a cruise aboard the Holland America cruise ship the Zuiderdam.

M. N. Vijayan, an Indian writer, orator and academic, died of cardiac arrest during a televised interview.

Miriam Makeba suffered a heart attack shortly after singing her hit song "Pata Pata" in a concert held in Castel Volturno, near Caserta, Italy.

American guitarist Mike Scaccia (Rigor Mortis, Ministry, The Revolting Cocks) collapsed on stage during a special Rigor Mortis performance in Fort Worth, Texas. Scaccia was taken to hospital, where he was pronounced dead. Cause of death was listed as a heart attack.

Mick Farren died on-stage at the Borderline, London, while performing with his band, The Deviants. The cause of death was stated to be a heart attack.

Italian singer Mango died from a heart attack during a concert in Policoro, province of Matera, while performing his song "Oro."

Mexican wrestler Perro Aguayo Jr. suffered fatal cardiac arrest caused by cervical spine damage during a match.

Former Megadeth drummer Nick Menza collapsed and died of heart failure during a performance with his band OHM at The Baked Potato in Los Angeles.

Taiwanese singer Kuo Chin-fa collapsed on stage when he just finished singing the first stanza of his best-known work "Hot Rice Dumpling" during a performance in Kaohsiung. He was then declared dead in a hospital of cardiorespiratory failure.

Guitarist and jam band performer Colonel Bruce Hampton collapsed and died of a heart attack during a jam at an all-star concert held in honor of his 70th birthday at the Fox Theatre in Atlanta, Georgia.

Laudir de Oliveira, Brazilian percussionist and former member of the band Chicago, died of a heart attack during a performance in Rio de Janeiro, Brazil.

Comedian Ian Cognito died of a heart attack during a show in Bicester.

Luchador Silver King was wrestling a match in Camden Town, London, England against Juventud Guerrera when he suffered a heart attack.

Juliano Cezar, Brazilian sertanejo singer, died of a heart attack during a concert in Uniflor, Paraná.

Adapted from Wikipedia

THE SORROW

They had a song for when they were below. *Down in the old sewers*, they sang, *for when we go below.*

They'd come two, three times this summer. The tunnel started back off the pebbly beach and reedy pond where all the kids would swim, a prelapsarian sink engulfed by mucky woods and rusty streams.

Minh was up front, and she held the light. She shielded the flame with her palm, though every so often it sputtered, a damp draft through the dark from a source they never would reach.

Tibs took up the rear. He preferred it when Minh led, it giving him time to think and watch and dawdle. He counted his fingers and the flicks of her candle, the mutter of her Vietnamese swears.

This time they were going deep. They were already deeper than they'd been before. No broken beer bottles and cigarette butts. The graffiti was gone, an insinuation of smoke.

Minh was sometimes the girlfriend of Tibs. They were 10—this first blush of love. *Down in the old sewers*, they said, *for when we've been below.*

1974

The winter sky is brilliant and blue. A wind blows heavily, pushing the boughs of the enormous loblolly pine.

Did you ever notice, my girlfriend says, how hidden inside such a brilliantly blue day is an equally brilliant black night?

This is a normal kind of comment for my girlfriend and she is used to me not understanding.

We are headed for the bar. It is three days after Valentine's Day. I have the idea we will drink a deep red cocktail of some kind, though I am unsure what that would be.

My girlfriend gets behind the steering wheel. She is wearing space leggings, with pictures of galaxies and stars printed across her thighs, knees. Her crimson dress is trimmed at the hem in a flat white lace.

We sit at the bar and make small talk with the bartender, who is very shy. He smiles a lot and always has a pint glass in his hands, even when he has no beer to draw. The glass gleams in the low blue light of the bar.

Do you think, my girlfriend asks, this bar is haunted by the color of wine?

I can't understand the question, and I say so to her, the pale blue light falling upon the hollow of her scented throat.

This is when she tells me her grandfather used to frequent this bar, 50 years earlier. He sat, my girlfriend says, at this very rail, this very same bar, sipping tumblers of chardonnay.

You're haunted by your grandfather? I say.

Out on the street there is the sound of bumpers colliding, headlights breaking, the shouts of a woman.

My girlfriend turns back to me. My grandfather, she says, was shot dead one white dawn in 1974.

Black Crow and Snow

My girlfriend says, Why is snow white?

I say, I'll look it up.

She says, Actually I'd rather not know.

We walk to the supermarket. We had to get rid of the car because to fix it was too expensive. Snow is falling in big, white bunches, coating our coats. By the time we get to the supermarket, we are covered in it, snow people.

At most supermarkets, the produce is first, and this supermarket is no exception. To the immediate left are the peppers, yellow and red and green. To the right are the oranges and lemons, then the apples in red, yellow, and green. There are the green leaf lettuces, broccoli, and cucumbers. Onions and potatoes. A long bank of bananas in a separate aisle.

My girlfriend says, Do we want hotdogs?

I say, Only the best kind. The cheap ones give me a stomachache.

We leave the supermarket with our four bags, each carrying two. My girlfriend stops halfway home, sets her bags on the cement, rummages through one.

What did you get? I say.

She shows me the Snickers bar she must have let slip into her bag.

Oh wow, I say.

Her eyes are big as she tears at the wrapper with her teeth. She is very pleased as she chews.

The snow is much finer now and the wind blows and the temperature has dropped. By the time we get home, the snow is not melting on the grass, there dusting it in white.

I say, It's very pretty.

Before we climb the stairs to go inside, she sets her bags on the cement one more time. She cocks one hip out to the side.

I say, How pretty you are.

She answers, Isn't it lucky?

I want to say, What is lucky? but I don't. I don't want to know.

My girlfriend leans forward to kiss me tremulously on the lips. The snow is swirling in the air, all about our heads.

My girlfriend says, I'm ready—

Just as a shining black crow croaks out from a tree.

He called himself The Misfit and he had a wooden leg. In fact, it was made of plastic but he'd wrapped it in wallpaper of the sort that might mimic a Tahoe rental. It was done of such skill that even the knotholes matched at the seams.

He liked to carry around a dusty Bible and stand in the square to read it out loud. Sometimes he wore a wide-brimmed preacher's hat and at other times a parrot-covered shirt, never mind the Margaritaville logo on the back.

He liked to think of himself as Saved. You, he'd say to the street kids under the freeway, their skateboards and spray paint in their hands. Will you join me at the right hand of God?

Fuck off, they answered, keeping themselves from reach. The Misfit was large and propulsive and all they wanted was to be left alone with their pills and whatever money they could inveigle on the corners.

On occasion though, when he had cigarettes, they might come near.

What are you? they wanted to know. Some kind of vet?

I don't like animals, he answered. They don't have souls for saving.

They sniggered. Not like that, they said. Afghanistan. Your leg.

Iraq, he said, and smiled. Like anyone he liked to be teased. By anyone he hoped to be loved by.

That's fucked up, said the boys.

He waved them off. Do you know why I call myself The Misfit?

They smoked his cigarettes and thought of their pills, untasted yet in their coats.

I call myself The Misfit because I'm the shattered appliance of God. I am crippled in His rage, handicapped of holy violence. And with that, he pulled a thrift-store steak knife from his pocket.

Dude, they said.

You'd have been good boys, he told them, if only there'd been someone to stab you every day of your lives.

A drip of greasy water fell from the overpass and onto his brow. It was late in the day, and he wobbled on his plastic leg. The boys came forward then and kicked him into the ditch.

The Council

The owl was tired of it. Why are we the indicator species? she said. Indicate this, motherfuckers.

Lol, said the coyote. I'd give a fifty-dollar bill to be an indicator. At least they don't shoot you for eating a cat or two.

They sat at the edge of the cornfield, Owl on a branch, Coyote on his haunches. The sun threatened to come out from behind the falling rain, extinguished itself again. Way off they saw the smoke rise from a tractor.

At that, a gray mink appeared, face like a wax mannequin, dragging her broken arm.

What's up with you? said the owl.

Trap, said Mink.

I know that, said Coyote.

A fourth joined, now in quorum, the dog with a Valentine on his forehead. He was known to love Man. Man was known to let Dog in the house—sometimes when it rained.

Hello, said the dog.

The owl sighed. The mink let out a whimper.

What say you? asked the coyote. Are you with us today?

Dog smiled. He had all the man's secrets. He knew where Man was weak. He knew that Man was not nearly weak enough. Yes, said the dog.

The tractor rumbled. The smoke bruised the rain.

Eleven Things My Mother Told Me

1. The average thickness of a boy's skull is less than that of bread.

2. Onomatopoeia is derived from the language of the Potawatomi.

3. Evolution is how humans descended from the flowers.

4. In 100 years mothers will be replaced with ditto machines.

5. Every story of fratricide has been grossly exaggerated.

6. Gravity pulls birds upwards towards the sun.

7. "Joey, I'm in love with Batman."

8. The tongue was the very first unit of measure.

9. Some babies turn out to be bowling balls.

10. The Little People cannot be lost.

11. If you hold your arms like that the trees will think you're growing.

Outside the window the rats struggle in the grass, squealing like an unhappy tennis match. My wife smiles at the sound; she figures it's nature.

She gets up to put her cake plate in the sink but stops halfway there to inspect something in the carpet.

Is that blood? she says.

I don't look at her, pretend I'm enjoying this *Smithsonian*.

She sets the cake plate next to the lamp and approaches. Bleeding? she wants to know. All over again?

It's nothing, I say, and my fingers reach for my nose. Just the weather's so dry.

She drops to a knee and puts her chin in my lap. Her nails pinch the seam in my pant leg. You're okay, she says, you're fine.

I don't tell her what I couldn't know. The rats play tennis, my wife smiles, the lamps burn.

Pledge

For Halloween Dave came as Cain and John as Abel. John had a bloody head and Dave carried around a palm-sized rock he'd found at the end of fraternity row. As things got drunker, the two would reenact the sin with deepening delight. I am NOT my brother's keeper! Dave would bellow, falling—laughing—to his knees.

In actuality, things were not so well between the two. Not in years. Nobody knew the vicious things they said to one another about their respective sizes, sexualities, politics, tastes in movies and music. Everybody around them had always said how nice it was that two boys so different were such pals.

As the party was winding down, John stood doubled-over next to the hot tub, barfing onto the cement. Dave, having just received sexual favors in one of the rooms upstairs, came out to take in the stars.

Hey, said one to the other.

Hey, said the other one back.

Hey, said a girl dressed as Satan, whom they hadn't seen in the dark.

The Pants

When my dad was a boy he knew a boy whose pants caught fire. The boy ran through the field screaming "I'm on fire!" The sun was headed down and behind the boy the pink sky was on fire as well. When my dad told this story I was a boy. We camped in the forest on the shore of the lake and in the falling dark we heard the shush of the waves on the sand. My sister, my dad, our shepherd, and I sat in a ring. Among us was the fire. My dad's hands were soft on his knees. His shoulders were cupped and curved. In the distance in the dark we heard the soft shush of the waves. In the distance we heard the shush of the waves.

[a wooded path above a lake]

Girl 1: Look, a lake.

Girl 2: Oh yes, it's a lake!

Girl 3: I didn't know there was a lake.

Girl 4: I've been to this lake.

Girl 5: Can you swim in this lake?

Girl 6: I want to swim in this lake!

Girl 7: You do realize this lake is polluted?

Girl 8: That lake is nasty.

Girl 9: That lake has snakes.

Girl 10: That lake is so weird.

Girl 11: That lake is so old.

Girl 12: That lake's not that old.

Girl 13: That lake is like 100 years old.

Girl 14: This lake is kind of cute.

Girl 15: I mean, most lakes are cute.

Girl 16: Most lakes are scary.

Girl 17: Except some lakes aren't scary.

Girl 18: This lake is really blue.

Girl 19: It's pretty green, this lake.

Girl 20: This lake is pretty small.

Girl 21: You couldn't swim across this lake.

Girl 22: This lake is cold.

Girl 23: This lake has changed.

Girl 24: This lake has potential!

Girl 25: This lake is ours!

Girl 26: This lake is mine!

Girl 27: This lake is everyone's!

Girl 28: I'll fucking marry this lake!!

[beat]

Girl 29: Should we go down to the lake?

Girl 30: I'll go down to the lake.

Girl 31: You aren't allowed to go down to the lake.

Girl 32: Does this lake belong to someone?

Girl 33: This is a rich person's lake.

Girl 34: This is such a poor person's lake.

Girl 35: This is an awesome person's lake.

Girl 36: This lake is a person.

Girl 36: Why can't a lake be a person?

Girl 37: This is totally a lake.

Girl 38: I like this lake.

Girl 39: I pretty much don't like this lake.

Girl 40: This lake is like, *What the shit?*

[beat]

[beat]

Girl 41: Dude, oh my god, this lake.

Greasy White and Blue Kittens

The city bus chuckled, wiggled, and smoked down the block, each 18 minutes, a greasy blue and white cat. They, the boy and girl, the twins, Allie and Hal, hazel-eyed and rosy, looked up from their algebra homework, into the other's face, and smiled. Each 18 minutes—for what was it?—11 years? Ever since, anyway, their bobbling baby-green eyes could locate a city bus among the general background blur. The city bus and the stolid men, the happy men, the worried and happy women, the children, the children, behind the greasy wide windows.

They were in trouble, Allie and Hal, because they were about to fail Algebra and no matter that it was quarter past nine, they were going to study, or else. We'll put trouble in scare quotes—like this: "trouble"—and "or else" too, since they'd never been in actual trouble since they were babies bobbling in the foregrounds of their parents' laps. They were both too sweet, too kind-eyed, too special, or when they were not any of these and were as grubby, cruel, and selfish as any kids can be, their parents—Debbie and Freddie—were clueless as to what to do. Debbie and Freddie, rosy-eyed and hazel, were talked about by most of the more competent parents on most of the block. No one was quite sure what was "wrong" with them. Though mostly, no one really cared, not really or not for long.

Allie and Hal called to their parents for pop. Can we have pop? they said. We're so thirsty, said one, for orange pop, said the other who had not yet spoke. At half past nine? answered one of their parents, as the other one set out the glasses. Thank you, said the twins, who really had not been ruined by the incompetence of their parents, no more ruined than any of the other children on most of the block, since all children eventually are ultimately ruined.

The city bus smoked and wiggled down the block, like a white and blue kitten, all the men and women behind the greasy wide windows. It was Allie, or Hal, or perhaps even one of their parents, who first had said that the city bus was a cat—a wandering, skittering, headlight-eyed cat. A cat! it was Allie or Hal who had said—10 or 8, or even 6 years ago. A beautiful and cute, blue and white cat!

All except now, at quarter past ten. Burned down from sucrose and homework, on the couch, the goldang numbers in the book, their parents more than ready for the absence of them, the twins looked away from the bus and into the other's eyes. They didn't, and wouldn't, couldn't smile, for tomorrow was another long day, and coming, and school was a treacherous sea, and couldn't they just go to bed? Couldn't they go to bed? Couldn't they—they asked Debbie and Freddie—just go to goddamn or goldang or ever-loving bed?

Objects I Keep Abusing

When the garbage truck is finished beeping in the alley

The little package that is a text from them

When the neighbor dog and my coffee are growling in my
spine

The moment before anyone thinks of what to do

Putting periods in the places that periods go

When the classroom falls like the green Atlantic waves

Did you hear that, dear, it was the furnace coming on

The patchouli all across the Pacific trail

When the power line starts burning in the alley

Your Mother the Minimalist

It looked like a box. It was white, and square. It sat in the parking lot, about 5 feet high, the same wide. From where they were they couldn't see if it had a top—that is, a way to get inside. Was it made of plaster? Or wood? Alabaster and gold?

He hated it. But she loved it.

What should we do tonight? he said.

I'd like to stay home, she answered.

What's for dinner then?

Steak?

Okay. With beer.

From the bathroom window they could see the box. The other tenants drove around it, to park, to leave. At night it gloamed a little and in the morning it was wet and shiny. Perhaps it was made of ivory and bone. Or plastic.

Now she hated it. But he was resigned.

They looked at each other and laughed.

The Perplexing Bumble Bee

The Perplexing Bumble Bee is the yellowest of all Maryland Bumble Bees, of which she is one of more than ten. That is, unless she's in the sun too long, as the bumblebee's soft coat can fade with the strong light. The buzz that gives the Bumble Bee her name shakes free the pollen in a flower and onto her body, to take home to the nest. The Perplexing Bumble Bee, like all Bumbles, can sting, though these bees are known, as a genus, to be gentle. The Perplexing Bumble Bee may fly into your house, seeming to look for something. What is she looking for, circling your legs, your room, bumbling in gentle loops? Quietly coax her outside again.

#bumblebee #pollinator #perplexing #soyellow
#maryland #citywildlife #urbananimals

The Song Sparrow

The Song Sparrow is a small brown bird. In Maryland, you might confuse the Song Sparrow with the Savannah Sparrow or Lincoln's Sparrow. You might even confuse the Song Sparrow with the House Sparrow, a chunkier bird that came from Europe. The Song Sparrow is a prolific singer, who can sing 20 different songs with 1000 variations. Some of their songs sound like Beethoven's Fifth. These Sparrows learn their songs from their neighbors and use these tunes to distinguish their neighbors from strangers. Song Sparrows employ cultural learning, passing what they know along the generations. You might learn to tell a Song Sparrow apart from his neighbor.

#songsparrow #brown #culturallearning #maryland #citywildlife #urbananimals

The Eastern Gray Squirrel

The Eastern Gray Squirrel is, as you might think, mostly gray. This Squirrel is crepuscular and so prefers to be out during the twilight hours of dusk and dawn, or when the day is gray. The name Squirrel comes from the Greek words *skia* and *oura*, or "shadow tail," referring to the habit of shading himself beneath his bushy tail if he happens to be out during a yellow day. The Eastern Gray Squirrel is much faster at making decisions than you are when driving your car. Be careful, and remember that most vehicular encounters with the Eastern Gray Squirrel result in no harm to any party. Squirrels have excellent spatial memory. They may only pretend to bury food if they think someone is watching. The Eastern Gray Squirrel hides a potent brain.

#easterngraysquirrel #becareful #graymatter #maryland #citywildlife #urbananimals

The Chimney Swift

The Chimney Swift had to change names. His flight is erratic. Chimney Swifts migrate to Peru when winter comes. He once lived in hollow trees. Chimney Swifts scare predators by making a collective thunder with their wings. A Chimney Swift rips off twigs in flight to build his nest. Audubon called the Chimney Swift the American Swift. The Chimney Swift eats airborne spiders. When the trees were cut down, the American Swift had to nest in chimneys. There is disagreement whether the Chimney Swift mates in flight. The chattering in your chimney could be baby Chimney Swifts. The species name, Pelagica, means "of the sea." Leave your chimney open for the Chimney Swifts. Chimney Swifts migrate in clouds of many thousands. It only looks like he beats his wings out of sync. The sooty-colored Chimney Swift is something that's fast.

#chimneyswift #americanswift #erratic #thatfast
#maryland #citywildlife #urbananimals

The Clover Mite

If you look on the internet, you'll see that the Clover Mite is widely considered a pest. In Maryland, they might gather on your garden wall to take in the sun; they might come inside to sit on your windowsill. Clover Mites do not harm your house, pets, or furniture. They do not bite. If you hurt them they leave a red stain. The Clover Mite is parthenogenetic. She lays her eggs and when they hatch they are genetically identical to her and her sisters. No one has ever identified a Clover Mite that's male. The Clover Mite receives her color from the plants she eats—clover, dandelion, daffodil. She is so small you might not notice her, tiny as the dot on an i.

#clovermite #innocuous #identical #i #maryland #citywildlife #urbananimals

The Turkey Vulture

As you know, the Turkey Vulture eats death. He's been known, through the study of his pellets, to feast on the carrion of mice, shrews, deer, pigs, sheep, chickens, blackbirds, snakes, turtles, shrimp, snails, grasshoppers, mayflies, coyotes, sea lions, and more. In Maryland, adjust accordingly. Maybe better to say the Turkey Vulture plucks death, the Latin word *vulturus* meaning to pluck or tear. The Turkey Vulture plucks the instrument of death, perhaps because in lacking a syrinx he can't sing. In flight, a flock of Vultures is a kettle, a roiling cauldron of soup as they ride the thermals above. The Turkey Vulture smells death. One of his kettle soars close to the ground to pick up the scent, alerting the rest to the body. Of the genus *Cathartis*, the Vulture is thus "the purifier." Lovely, ugly, essential, the Turkey Vulture is the cleaner of death.

#turkeyvulture #intodeath #likesagoodbody #lovely #maryland #citywildlife #urbananimals

The Mockingbird

Mokkinbado o kiku. Ting zhi geng niao. Escute o mockingbird. Luister na die bespotting. Ascolta il mockingbird. Samleng saechchmak. Makinig sa nakakatawa.
Gwrandewch ar y gwatwar. Hern tsu di mokingbird.
Mockingbirdni tinglang. Listen to the mockingbird. Lytt
til hanfuglen. Horen Sie sich den Spottdrossel an. Isma
'l-mockingbird. Auskultu la mokridulon. Fa'alogo I le
tauemu. Akouste to koroidevo. Koute mockingbird la.

#mockingbird #mimuspolyglottos
#mimicofmanytongues #googletranslations #maryland
#citywildlife #urbananimals

The Eastern Eyed Click Beetle

You may be tempted to write about the Eastern Eyed Click Beetle, since he's so handsome, but you've never seen him in person. Write about *Aeolus sp.*, who you have, and is pretty easy on the eye in any case. *Aeolus sp.*, like all Click Beetles, clicks. Should a Bird or Human come upon him in the grass, he'll fall to his back, playing dead. Touch him with a beak or finger and the special spine on his thorax will snap to send him into the air, and several inches away, with an audible click. This sudden change in locale may help him to click another day. Nice work, *Aeolus sp.* Aeolus was the Greek god of the wind, "The Changeable," which sounds about right. The Click Beetle is cosmopolitan, with a range over much of the world. You may write about him wherever you are.

#aeolus #clickbettle #notthatonetheotherone #maryland #citywildlife #urbananimals

The Evening Bat

The Evening Bat is fond of the evening. Whether she is more fond of the evening than other Bats, almost all of whom are nocturnal, is an interesting thing to consider. Female Evening Bats are quite social. They gather in maternal colonies of up to 300 individuals as they raise their pups. They recognize their pups by their individual smells and their individual squeaks. Being a mammal, an Evening Bat nurses her pups with her milk, and she might nurse pups she did not birth as well. Evening Bats display resource partitioning, deciding to eat different insects than other Bats to limit the competition for food. Since flying takes so much energy, requiring a strong flow of blood through her body, a Bat's heart is three times larger than most mammals. The Evening Bat is fond of the beetles that eat our crops. Some of us are not fond of Bats, which is an interesting thing to consider.

#eveningbat #nosesthatlooklikedogs #3xheart #maryland #citywildlife #urbananimals

THE PLATYPUS

I've never been to New Zealand, but that doesn't mean I'm not an expert. I've never shot the Queen either, but that doesn't mean I won't.

In New Zealand, you know, they have the platypus. The platypus has a goose bill, a muskrat tail, and snake venom in its foot. It keeps its baby in its pouch—hoppity-hop.

How do you find your prey if you're a platypus? Electrolocation. I can hear ya muscles, mate! That's what they say in New Zealand.

The Queen is queen of New Zealand. I wish they'd get rid of her. All she does is muck about, waving her little hand. My father and my father's father were peat farmers in the way-back times. They hated the wee lass. They were practically her slave.

My grandmother, she hated violence. She stood firmly on its head—would not send her boys to fight. This not discounting the beatings my grandfather gave her. I never met the son of a bitch, peat fork, peat hat, peat hands, peat eyes.

My granddaughter is coming this afternoon. She loves the animal book. She starts at the aardvark clear through to the zebra. She says it like Debra. The Zebra called Debra. We linger over the platypus too: What a charmer.

Grandpa? Would you save me if someone tried to nap me? She looks at me with one eye. I can't have anybody nap me. What she says when she means kidnap. Why she hollers when it's time to sleep.

Darling, I would never let them. I am your knight in armor. They would not, could not, dare.

She looks at me skeptically, with only one eye. Grandpa, they always do. *Always*.

What a strange beast—bioluminescent in the dim afternoon room—and I am in love.

Everything is Interesting, Everything is Good

She was upset that people called them boring bees. Typical bio-phobia, she said, irises tipping toward the moon. *You're boring*, she followed hypothetically.

In the morning, she made waffles. Her waffles had jalapenos embedded amongst them.

I asked her, Is there syrup?

I don't like it, she said.

I do.

From the far back of the cupboard she rummaged a bottle of the best kind.

Swell, I said.

She stuck out her tongue. She stuck out her unclad hip.

In 4 hours she was watching a show on music. The bands comprised a pretty boy and a pretty girl or two, a couple shlumpy ones as well. The shlumpy ones were sometimes the frontperson and the pretty ones were sometimes the drummer.

Do you like these bands? she asked, as I waltzed through the room.

I don't know these bands.

Do you like this band? she said, pointing at the TV.

I nodded and she smiled and was not-so-secretly pleased with my answer.

We were in bed, perhaps about to have sex. It's not because they are boring people, I said. The bees, I mean. The bees aren't boring people.

She slid her shirt over her head so her breasts shined at me. I know, she answered. Because, she said, they are also called carpenter bees. They bore.

Okay, I said.

When I was a girl, a boring bee would follow me about the yard. It knew me and I it.

She drew off her panties and I kissed her willing throat.

The small girl was at play in the yard. The big tree that dropped green nuts was Grandma. Grandma held out her fingers and to them the bluejays and sparrows flew. The sparrows bounced and nattered: seed-d-ds, sk-k-ky, impending autumn-tumn-tumn. The jays shouted at the cat: Free, free! They were exultant, vain and intolerably blue.

In the fall the small girl went to school. Her teacher, Ms. Great, was terribly advanced. Ms. Great told the truth. Even and especially to children.

The birds sing for their territory, she said. The trees outgrow their neighbors for light. The cat is cruel for its kittens.

The small girl, now older, was at work in her freshman labs: A petri dish of river life. She recalls the lessons of the formidable Ms. Great. All the words of her teacher, her teacher's teacher, her teacher's teacher's teacher. The long, white cataracts of knowing.

The small girl, now old, sits in her yard. It's been a time of science. A nice life, and she has been kind. A hard life, and she was kind. She took so many awards, wrestled so many honors. At the corner of her eye, Grandma shakes a finger. A squirrel laughs something in French.

THE MURDER

You hear about the murder? Danny's eyes were on his phone, a text from his girl.

Naddie shrugged. Same old, he said.

Except for the face. Cut clean off.

Dead is dead. Naddie shrugged again.

Behind the boys was the park, a couple soot-streaked trees sending weak leaves at the sky. A black squirrel "stood" on the trunk, near vertical, head toward the ground. The sun was in its dark fur so to make each tip of hair a licorice light, a thousand and a half. It looked towards the boys, watched their heads and hands, dark eyes alight like the fur. In its dark brain a thousand stars of light flashed in sequence, to feet, to tail, to heart, to nose, to eyes, to teeth, to throat, to gut, to brain again.

The squirrel considered the boys, their heads and hands. The tip of a head might signal their intention, to cross the street between them and the park, to find a stone on the ground to throw, to reach into a pocket for something sweet to eat. The hands followed the head a perceptible moment later, made such threat or enticement complete. The squirrel was a dial to the boys' sun.

In a perceptible moment the squirrel would jump to the ground to look for a nut or potato chip. Or turn to climb the tree again from which to look out across the park, the street, the boys, the buildings, and into the sky. The squirrel sought the sky as any climbing creature might.

I'm out, said Danny, and readied to leave.

Naddie considered his mother. She was three years gone and he missed her so.

The Paintings of Forrest Bess

Spots (1967)

Because we began here, of sods in the mind, he sat on his hot water pier. This was or was not Texas, all lowering of pelican and gull. What fish may be best? What parts, heads or fin? Do you have the simple worm? Ah great god, you've sent vision of the natural sky. Ah I am in love. Oh sorry that I am. Build clear to this ache in my eye.

The Dicks (1946)

What do we already see, this wet horizon? This a man, this a paint. They shimmer, the dicks, oh uncontrollable. Still so sure and still, taking up the margins, waiting for the hurricanes on the marsh.

The Warrior (1947)

At the elbow of the brain, walking there. I fight the alligators and minotaurs, the lesser halves of women. You see the rough-turned wire? You see the hooks in the head? You see the tar of the mouth? You see the fresco of fingernail? You see the white a-boil? You see the substrate that can't be smoothed? You see the cabin there in the sand? All of these.

Untitled (1951)

There up on the mount, the number, the legion, light. Slate has run wet and dry, eyed. Take us back now, dead, take us up. These dim cables of Gotham.

Untitled #31 (1950)

That dream over a night sky, same and different, the ordinary tooth of it. Remember hands of sand? The cupidity of hills? We were all there then, dad and I, this head not broken. Whereof the cracks send down light to light the unlit. That it does something to a body.

And all the things I have forgotten (1953)

You are frightened? You are. You are frightened? You are. Take these great ark. Take these great ark for covenant with dirt. For blasphemy of covenant of dirt.

Mandala (1955)

Sea grape and grape shot, the seed of the 17th god, barra-
cho la playa enfermos. You see me now. Ears four points,
three winds and a gale. The fog shall drop and we all lie
low. The fish do skim their own bright skiffs.

Drawings (1957)

I think we can tell you 5 things: that the sea spins, that the
god will die, that the wires of the head shall sing, that an
old man takes breath, that we look to see the enveloped
beauty of souls.

Gold mountain (1966)

Perhaps here at the end, fell down and shy, the lifting of
eyes, a great shield of signs. It's only a paint, a man. Build
now to the ache in the hand. Wherever the gold says, we
will have to, have to go.

Cambrian Explosion

She had an idea for a TV show about two deer running through the woods. The deer were telepathic of course and though they were running from a hunter, they had a long, silent discussion about human ontology, which neither deer is sure we have.

And that's the whole show? he asked. How is that a show?

She shrugged. There's drama, characters, and an idea. How is that not a show?

She typed up the pilot and he edited it. One thing is that she kept switching the names of the two deer around, with the browner deer sometimes being identified as Flo and sometimes as Lucy. And vice versa, naturally.

I wanted that, she said. That's part of the show.

He sadly lowered his gaze. How is that part of the show?

It's the plot.

She sealed up the pilot and sent it to David Simon. She used all of the stamps left in the house. He wanted to say that David Simon wrote TV, he didn't produce it, but he was sure she had an answer to that as well.

In six months, David Simon called her. He wanted to discuss the show's setting. He felt that the deer should run through a field of tall grass and shrubs, rather than a forest. Otherwise, David had no notes.

What's the name of this show? he asked, thoroughly confused, deeply chagrined. Is it still untitled?

No. *Cambrian Explosion.*

He yelped. How is that the name of a show?

That's when you went from a little of something to a whole lot of something—the explosion. That's the show's emotional heart.

This hurt as much as anything else, and he hurt a lot, but he was beginning to see that maybe she was right. This was the golden age of everything.

POLITICS

She wanted pizza but we didn't have the money. That's why the bread and spaghetti sauce were gone. That's why we didn't have anything to make when the neighbors came over.

Who are you going to believe, John the neighbor was saying. A cattle rancher, or the president of the U.S.?

I could hardly keep up with the tenor of this conversation. Who were we supposed to side with, was what I couldn't follow. Maybe John was a nationalist. Or maybe he was just hungry.

Pickles, my girlfriend, decided to get out the guitar. She had a song that flushed out intransigents.

> *The Indian that cries, it's the woman*
> *The paupers that cry, it's the women*

John and his wife Katie stopped looking at their hands. Katie opened her mouth into a lovely O. O, she said. Her eyes were blue.

Damn, John answered. Goddamn. He was angry, but I couldn't tell the tenor. Was he mad at me and Pickles, or was he mad at Katie?

That rancher had over 10,000 cows! he said. Can you see what I'm saying?

I wanted to run to Katie. I wanted to take her away. Protect her. I wanted all of this and every world.

THE WALL

They've been working on the wall next door for 6 months. Pounding, scraping, sanding—what in hell could they be building? How many nails can a wall hold before nails is what it is?

This thing you ask me, you say, So what about it? Why should I care?

And I answer, Because you're God.

And you say, Oh! Flattery!

The pigeons swirl through the air, a funnel of feathers and blue sky. A man with a big, stiff dog puts a handkerchief to his mouth and wrinkles his forehead. Disease, he says to me, with some pleasure in his eyes.

You think it's me? you say. I do these things?

If not you, I answer, Who? Who puts blue light in the sky, infection in the air? Who is behind the hand behind the wall?

The toast comes up as golden as sunlight when I prefer it black.

You look for ideas where there's only matter, you say. It's
dull. How dull.

I say, Even God fails to know what's within his skull, working in secret.

You laugh, so hard the trees spread their leaves, the roses
begin to grow.

In flash fiction let's disremember our character. There she is—the little girl or grandmother or scientist—since this is her story, but perhaps let's let her fade into a sepia of the warm and sun-worn story. Perhaps let us see our writer, her hot sensate fingers, her consciousness a golden flower burning the words about her into dust.

In flash fiction, make your plot of open air, a late November field where the rain is ice and the ice rattles on the milkweed pod. There is such expanse, this story, a thousand Russian Novembers, a two-wheeled cart pulled by a very old goat. We're finally out of the city and our shoulders open out.

In flash fiction: a place where everyone is given what they need, a utopia of badgers and buildings. I met a man today. He said, the world is as soft as lace.[a]

In flash fiction follow your rules. Your ledger is green and full of marks that tell you how you've done. The admiral always points his fleet in the direction of battle. Tell your story and then tell it again. Again. All of you get one story.

In flash fiction, the tree or pretty person is that through which you shoot the arrow. To strike at what? Something. Anything. Nothing? I alone am aimless and depressed.[b]

I think it's always time to go to sleep in flash fiction. At the far back of your brain is an ocean and everyone knows the waves are setting you to sleep. You may want to stay up to see the show, but flash fiction is in charge of things now. You're about to slip under so go on seal shut your pretty eyes.

a   Belle and Sebastian

b   Lao Tzu

Of All the Creatures These Are the Creatures That Talk the Most

Box Turtle

Some say that we are shaped like the pond upside-down: This is why we left the pond a long time ago. Some others say that we resemble the sky: That's why we live so long. Either way, it's not much important to us: Brand us your God or forgo us your teasing. One grub is as keen as the next.

May Apple

We wait to see who will have a white flower, whose will be yellow, and who will have no flower at all. It was once a contest among young Mays which flower or no flower they would turn out to be, but the habit has been abandoned. It's a custom we left behind just as our fruits discard their poison as they mature. Poison or no, flower of one kind or none, it's all gone down in the long years of summer, passed in a thousand years.

Pill Bug

At night beneath the log—and all time is night beneath the log—we sing to the eggs. Yes, to our eggs—the capsule of our future children—but equally to the eggs of spiders and newts. We sing songs of all eggs awakening. It's quiet in the midnight world, and we sing songs of eggs awakening.

Woodpecker

A story we tell is of the three days that our woods were visited by the men in red. They were tired and hungry, many bled from their hands or heads. In those days men had no machines, none except the carts drawn by animals in chains. The red the men were dressed in was as bright as feathers, and though there was mostly fright in their eyes and pain in their calls we found them to be beautiful—as one might in flight across the pond, looking to the referent surface below.

Beaver

In the river we float. Ice river, autumn river, green river. We make our dams and caution our children, we argue with the woodchuck, but mostly we float. What a thing to float.

Dog

This is not my home, down by the weedy ravine, and it is my home. This is not my home, in the midst of the daisies, and it is my home. This is not my home, where the bears used to go, and still it is my home. I am a dog—I meet you there.

Elm

We don't mind if the bugs eat our bark, and we don't mind if the deer browse our leaves. We don't mind if rot comes too soon, and we don't care if we lose a limb. But it isn't true that we don't mind a thing. We mind when the spring is too long, and we care when the men come along. We don't mind when the winds are too rough, but we mind when the soil is traced with salt. No: Don't believe we are the grandmothers of virtue. Don't believe we are uncles of care.

Human

We are always holding hands. We take up the grip of joy or violence. We hold hands with one another. We've forgotten how to hold the hands of eagles or fish. We make and remake the world. We're tired. We do like to play with our hands.

Nervous-Ghosts; or, The Utilities of Wonder

This is the magical part: at night, should the moon be out at all, he could watch the bunnies leap over the green-black lawn, a guardian of bats tying the night into complicated shoes.

This is the realist part: he had no legs from the knee down, being as he was from one of the countries with landmines as numerous as rabbits. Oh though he did have shoes— his collection of wingtips of red-wine and gold.

He slept mostly through the mornings. He hated the man from Meals for Those Without Heels who arrived each day with his breakfast and his indefatigable charm. He hated the man as much as he loved him, as who who were human would not?

His neighbor, Gladys Permafrost, a fourteen-year-old girl with orange-eyeshadowed eyes, came at noon. Pretty soggy stuff, she would inevitably say, lifting the Styrofoam lid to peak at the wiggling of eggs inside. Toast as stiff as panicky ghosts.

Thank you, Miss Permafrost, he answered, the formality of his country towards the company of strangers and always the offspring of neighbors.

Oh jesus, she invariably would say. Like, I'm a kid. Like, a kid.

She was the only one he would speak to over weeks at a time and he adored her all awkward elbows and sighs.

You are like a kid, he said—the only teasing he might manage.

But like, what's the deal? she said. Like, the Meals guy? Like, he's pretty nice?

Across his face and to his elbows a blooming of roses, the most embarrassed of almost inaudible moans.

Oh! she said.

He shook his head.

But? she said.

No, he answered.

But maybe? she said.

I have to eat, he said. Goodbye, Miss Gladys. Bye-bye. He suffered a smile and showed her the door.

This is the realist bit: the world is grey and blue and orange and all the shades of violet and green. It shows up like light on a screen.

This is the magical bit: he waited for morning as the kit foxes called as across the deep his legs stay asleep in the ground.

BLUE RIDGE

Ray had to get his beagle across the river, and we kept shouting to him from the bottom of the waterfall. Ray! we said. That stone's loose. My god, Ray, be careful, while Poky hung limp in his arms, licking her long teeth, her big blue heart beating in cadence with his. Over their heads, we saw the pines that swung in the sky, roots touching rock that touched the roots of the mountains.

We met Ray back at camp, a flat space between stones. We'd set cooking pots in the crooks of hemlocks and laid damp shirts over the bushes, until it was something like ours. Wherever we spilt water, the forest looked up at us to grin.

Ray, we said, How's Poky? and he pointed at her, sleeping in the weeds. We saw the long, deep gash up Ray's leg that still dripped blood. But we wouldn't mention that. He'd be angry and embarrassed.

We ate scrambled eggs and pepperoni and sat back to smoke. The woods gathered close, shimmered, and the river we couldn't see through the trees chimed. Our hands made interesting animals.

Finally, Poky woke with a whimper. She raised her head to look at us and smile. Ray, she's happy you saved her.

He fiddled with his shoes, his belt buckle. That old dog, he said.

You're her hero.

But he just spat, leaned back to look at the tops of the trees, the golden birds flickering in the lichen.

Ecological Study of a Bat Colony in the Tropical Rain Forest of Peru

On Christmas Eve 1971, Koepcke flew. Koepcke dealt with insect bites and a maggot in her arm. Sometimes called *The Story of Juliane Koepcke*. Those each side of Koepcke a parachute.

In Koepcke's case, experts credit. Koepcke herself still strapped to her seat. Having been widely, Koepcke's experience is the subject.

While in the jungle, Koepcke after 9 days. Koepcke assisted the bodies of victims.

Koepcke as "a kind of therapy." Koepcke last minute change. Koepcke published her thesis.

Art Cop

My girlfriend wanted to take pictures of me in the graveyard. She had her old Brownie.

That's stupid, I said. What a cliché.

Come on, George. Don't be such an Art Cop.

She dressed me in one of her dead grandfather's formal shirts, pearl buttons and ruffles, over 60 years old. There were pieces of bone in the collar–for chrissake–to keep it stiff.

You think these are chicken, I said, or human?

She rolled her eyes. Whales. Now quit stalling and stand by that tombstone, the one that says *The Blood Family*.

I did and she snapped a half dozen, one with my cheek pressed against the cold marble.

Yeah, now close your eyes, halfway. Not like that. Hooded, you dink!

When we were done, she kissed me. Was that so bad?

I nodded. Really bad.

Well, when we get these back, you'll see how cool they are.

The sun went down and the moon came up, round and colored like teeth. It was ridiculous.

June Cobb

The sisters, Elana and Deva, were urbane and charming, their house immaculately conceived. That last was a joke, one the sisters had told her: How angry their architect had been, after such a Christmas party 20 years past, Nacimiento, roaring and drunk, to see his creation in shambles. They were considerate hosts, the pair of them, literate and suave. She did not know how the cat's legs had been broken, twisted at the malleolus. As she told it, It hadn't been her.

She was hungry, and how she hated to make her own lunch. In Colombia, before the disease, its sores, the maids-of-all-work brought her sandwiches and pastry. There was a bell made of nickel, but she preferred to call to them through the archways, the walls of cream plaster. In New York, her voice was never so musical. English was a language of grunts.

They wanted to speak to her again—Congress. The Some Such Committee of Something. What they didn't know were her secrets, though they knew almost everything else: the white escarpments of cocaine, the love affair with Castro, Oswald's book, the beach house in Port Aransas. They, nor anyone, would know her secrets.

One of the two sisters, the one with fair hair, though she was known for her stories, angry and strange, wrote poems as well. She'd smuggled them out of the house, once— after the incident with the cat—the sisters had ordered her to leave. In trade she'd been a translator:

> All year is winter next to you,
> King Midas of the snow.
>
> …

She was working on it. She was always working. There was no end to it, one job after another after another. She could have remained home, in Ponca City. She could have planted corn or worked at the refinery. In such dissipate states of mind, she dreamt of Standing Bear. Of Prairie Flower and Bear Shield. Fanny Bear and Zazette. Cholera and buffalo.

One of the sisters was— Well, no more of that. She wouldn't go on—with hate, or in love, jealousy or regret, desire and disgust.

She was hungry. There were saltines in the cupboard. Saltines and apple butter. Apple butter and wine. She'd not be ashamed for this, of anything. There was movement to do. She was the antelope on the Oklahoma hills. She was secrets and blood, the revolutions, the assassinations, intrigue and perfidy, the screwdrivers to the joints, that men—always men—asked of her.

The Spanish Acre

At midnight the hare made her survey. She marched from post to grave, grave to ash, ash to creek, creek to post. Within this measure were her 14 living leveret, the wolves of prairie, the moon silverside, the moon, the prairie, the horse, tábano, her heart and feet, death, and at dawn a man with the harrow.

Applause Please

An elephant was in the upstairs room, the attic. She stood as elephants will, swaying trunk, beautiful eyes, pitched roof and rafters. Among her were the usual boxes and broken lamps.

Danae was cooking waffles—flour, baking soda, salt. Tim came in bearing the smell of snow and sat patiently at the table.

Cold out? said Danae. The phone said it would be dropping.

Tim's hands laced patiently on the tabletop. For sure, he said. A pinch in the lungs cold. Frozen mustache cold.

From the cleft of his chin, Danae saw a globe of water fall. It took the silver of the winter light and landed on his shirtfront button.

How's she doing? Tim said, eyes turned toward the ceiling.

Calm, she answered. Very calm.

Same then, he said.

Same as ever, she nodded.

This elephant is not a metaphor. She has nothing at all to do with the thoughts, wonders, and loves of Tim and Danae. She—as god or the empty stars allow—is her own elephant outright.

Danae set a plateful of waffles in front of Tim. She sat with her own.

Grace? she said.

Tim nodded and Danae began. Tim and Danae are not like you and me.

After breakfast, the light began to fail. The gray of the day turned to black, the clouds receded, and the winter stars appeared. It was 10 a.m.

Would you like a cup of coffee? said Tim. Another, I mean?

Okay, she said. She was frightened, but calm.

Are you frightened? she said.

I am, he answered.

In the morning dark, the elephant upstairs sounded her call—the first for her. It filled the house and then the black and snow-filled yard.

This is a movie, Tim said. A terrible movie.

Yes, Danae replied, I don't know. She was named for the famous painting by Klimt, for which some had called her parents obscene.

In the room, she readied herself—a second coming of day? I love you! she said, to someone in the room.

Markus was one afternoon lying on his couch with not much to do. He might have been working at the dry cleaners that day but he'd begged off sick. In fact, there was a touch of nausea in his stomach, but this was more spiritual infection than anything of the figure. He wouldn't have said so to his boss.

In any case, Markus was supine. He was, in other words, indolent. He was, as one would say, goldbricking, a rounder. This is important.

From his place on the couch—crimson with a yellow afghan thrown over its back—he faced the one window in the room. The window had no curtain but it did have a shade, one of those rollers the color of parchment.

Markus was not reading, since then in his life he had no interest in books. His friends talked about Camus and Camus and Camus, and Weil, but he hadn't a clue what they wrote. Cumbersome things that might have been beautiful, had he'd checked, he thought. If he had any interest, he thought, he might have been struck.

The rainy afternoon light came through the shade: two rectangles of almost equal dimension, one stacked above the other, transected at the center, the light parchment-colored and soft, dim but brightest at the middle, spectral to the edges, diffusely aglow, phantomic, psychic, transected at the center.

Markus never wanted to go back to the cleaners. It gave him incorporeal turns in his gut. What would he do? So holy, so precious, so lazy. What could he do?

The world was faintly and perfectly dizzy. He closed his eyes and there in the dark he hunted—he laid out—for form.

A New Practical Treatise on
the Three Primitive Colours
Assumed as a Perfect System of
Rudimentary Information

Sometime in the 80s someone placed a pane of purple glass in the window above the tool bench. Should you look from the top of the basement stairs, the rough, downstairs hollow seemed aglow, amethyst over much of the day, turning towards rose as the low sun of late afternoon put its rays between the houses.

Amarie was not a charity case, nor a cause célèbre, no matter how many neighbors argued whether food should be left at her doorstep or that her house was a magnet for rats, bats, and neighborhood cats and should so be condemned. They all could whisper in their sleeves; Amarie was an artist.

In the brilliance of morning, she sat on her porch, wide-eyed at the wig of moss greening phosphorescently on the roof across the street, at the dirty rock of pigeons a-strut in the gutter, the spokes of some girl's bicycle flashing hearts and diamonds as she rode past.

Amarie was an artist, and the hunger that gnawed at her spine only lifted the visions out of her liver and into her brain. She saw charts and wheels, Ezekiel's skies, the specs of papier mâché palaces from all the World's Fairs. Everything that sat between her temples was as master-piece and brilliant as the black rat pinned in the jaws of a common orange cat.

Something About Easter, Maybe

I was writing a poem about the blue sky and wind in my window. How wayward the early spring can be, rain and wicked, the sun and the damnable changing sky. Isis wanted nothing of it. Her tail flicked into my computer screen, claws in my chest.

Until the mouse across the kitchen floor, sprite and gray.

I watched her scramble, crouch, pounce. She's 19 but the mouse had no chance.

Get it, Isis, I cheered.

She danced about the house, its wavering tail in her mouth. She dropped it, battered it, clamped her teeth on its soft body. The mouse squealed—if that's what it can be called in its last kicks of life—squealed or squeaked or cried.

Good work, Isis, I said, though then not so sure. Oh, Isis, I said, her proud cat ways.

I went back to my poem. I made the sun a little warmer, the wind-blown branches agents in their own right.

Isis jumped into my lap, tired. You're old, I said. Nice job, cruel cat.

There was no more writing that day. The sun was headed down, thunder was in the east.

Is the **Black Place** Gray?

Far out the windshield it was a flat sand-blue to a horizon, then the trapezoid bump of a rock. The bump captured the lower left of the picture and she watched it swim.

Are we going there? she said.

He looked up from the speedometer which had been reading 90, 94, 85, 100. Not specifically? he said. Though maybe generally?

She whistled in her teeth in the way that he liked. We might be able to climb it, she said.

They did drift toward it, generally, with sometimes cactus lying in the sand-blue and then again a cow. The sun slanted on them from a moderate height.

They pulled to the shoulder, squeezing the car into the dust. She got out and tried to measure its distance. Do you think a mile? she said.

He squeezed his own shoulders. I have no idea. The bump was, more or less, bigger than when they first spotted it, an hour earlier. In no definite manner.

Well, we might as well try, she said. She went to the fence line and tested the barbs with her finger. With some resolution, she pulled apart the strands and bent through.

He stayed on the shoulder and watched her shrink against the not changing bump. Neither the sky changed as well.

A Pair of Men

A man goes to the supermarket and stands in the yogurt aisle, 8 feet long. He knows they don't have his brand so he buys his least favorite kind. He takes it home, puts it in a bowl, and does not eat it.

A second man sits in his threadbare chair. He has no money. He has no friends. He watches the white light of the day cast through the window and play on his floor.

The second man takes a bus downtown to sit in the park. The first man in his new shirt sits next to him. The two men watch children and pigeons and the dogs strut.

Do you live nearby? says the second man.

The first man points at the high rise rising past the trees.

Nice digs, says the second man.

The first man laughs. I prefer the country.

The second man laughs as well. Take what you can get, I suppose.

I suppose I don't want what I can get, the first man answers.

The two men watch a woman walk by who wears ruffles about her neck. She looks into her phone and smiles. She neither sees nor not sees the two men on the bench.

Are you married? the second man says.

Eleven years. He holds back a yawn. He wishes not to speak. You?

No. I once was. In fact, 11 years ago.

Hmm, says the first man. Lucky, I suppose.

The second man laughs. Well, she died, he says.

Lucky, I suppose, the first man says again.

The second man feels his anger rise. That's unkind, he says. He wants to hit the first man, and he does—he knocks the well-appointed shoe from where it rests across the first man's lap.

The first man looks at his knuckles. He does not want to apologize. My apologies, he says.

The second man shakes his head. He watches the light fall through the trees to play on the ground. Okay, he says, all right.

She had a show Saturdays, very late. In the booth, the band stickers, band graffiti, the unwashed smell of bands, piles of records, enormous ashtray. The record room was dark since all she needed was her book. The hallways were dark—stale, dark, and linoleum.

He left her, her boyfriend, the night before. Gotten from bed, dressed, clanged through the iron gate. In some moments, the streetcar—rattling close, braked. She thought of him climbing the steps, chunking change into the slot, sitting in the fluorescence, the plastic bucket of his seat.

She'd had a show Saturdays three years. Presumably it was for the blind, though anyone could listen. Who would listen? Of anyone awake, blind or not? *She would,* she would say—the damp of her palms, behind her knees, her ears, beneath her bra.

He was the most handsome man, boy, androgynoid she'd ever slept with. She quavered. The lust or love she felt tasted like blood and copper, stranger metals than that. He fucked her like a horse, dentist, waitress, tuna fish in love.

By the time she'd finished Saturdays the light had leaked through the streets, onto the bay. Or were it winter, the sun was still hours away. The streetcars underground and the push of air before you saw them, the smell of old paint and rags.

She hadn't started, yet. Four minutes of dead air since the last DJ had left, waved through the window, switched off the light in the record room she wouldn't need. Dead air, clammy shirt, the lugubrious excitement.

She toggled the switch, now open air. She read but didn't introduce—not herself, the book, the title, the giddy quiver, the this, the sad of it: *We cannot know his legendary head / with eyes like ripening fruit*

Princess Cecilie Viktoria Anastasia Zeta Thyra Adelheid of Prussia

Uncle Binn works at the helium reserve. Basically, he handles a wrench, loosening and unloosening things all the day long. A billion meters of gas! he's prone to say, his voice rising to a hilariously high pitch.

Auntie Binn dreamt of being a country music star. In her dream she wore an all-yellow Nudie Suit, carried a yellow guitar, called herself The Amarillo Rose. Pretty sure I woulda done it, she says. I had the sweetest voice. That was before Cousin Binn, the sweetest brain-damaged boy you'd ever meet.

Me and Cousin Binn go out to the Ranch. Now that I got my license, it's easy for us. We slide out at evening time, when I get off from work, as the sun sits down on the prairie. It's not the Cadillacs we go out to see—neither of us cares a whit. It's the hot wind, or the thunderheads off west, or the coyotes trotting home with jackrabbits in their jaw.

Cousin Binn can say No, Yes, Hungry, and Tired. He has trouble with Hungry, cries when he's Tired, teases his sister with No, eyes spark like winter with Yes. Yes is his favorite. Yes, yes, and yes, all the day long.

Everyone calls Cousin Binn Cousin Binn and his sister is Sister Binns. Sister Binns is two years younger and she is a jar of whoop de doo fuck. When the pastor said Halloween is a sin she rushed home to work on her costume. For three years running she's been Princess Cecilie Viktoria Anastasia Zeta Thyra Adelheid of Prussia.

Mom says Cousin Binn won't be around too long. It's a wonder, she says, we've had him as long as we have. Some people say it's because of the factory for nuclear bombs. Some people say some people have brains full of shit.

Cousin Binn and I go out to the Ranch. I hope he stays around until I'm done with school. What with that and the job I don't have enough time. We wander into the prairie and stand by a tangle of butterweed. After four years, there's hope that rain could fall. Cousin Binn is happy. He angles his arm to touch me in the ribs.

ORIENTATION

Each of his new teachers delivered a small speech. Orientation, they called it, welcome to junior high.

Math, said his math teacher, is everywhere. Everything you can think about comes back to math.

Once you see it, said his science teacher, you can't unsee it—science is the language of life, the planets, even love.

His social studies teacher said that the clock of history, of time itself, ran on sociology.

Ah music…, said the band teacher, waxing prophetic.

He went home at the end of his day. Of course he had to, had to, think of what his teachers had told him. Elementary school was gone. The classroom had exploded, all the world and its one teacher in its four white walls.

He played with his dog. Dog dog dog, said the dog. He pet his cat. Cat cat cat.

He grew tired of thinking and went outside. The end of summer was in the green droop of the leaves. The ants across the sidewalk were with a new urgency. His friends in the vacant lot wore socks and shoes and fresh cut hair.

Helllllo! he said and clapped them on the back. They gathered around a small pile of paper, burning in a shallow hole in the dirt.

Where did you get it? he asked, the girl with the can of lighter fluid.

Took it out of my dad's shed, she answered.

They watched the paper green, then orange, then black as the fire fed.

Someone threw in the plastic lid of a soda cup and they watched it melt and drip. Someone threw in a tuft of a dead squirrel's hair and they watched it fizzle and stink.

What about a rock! one of them said, and they all laughed as he tumbled it in.

He went home for dinner, some TV, and then to bed. He lay under the sheet and thought of fire and the feverous world. He smiled and laughed—until he saw the moon in his window. Where the sun that lit its face? Where the sea its gravity pulled?

He became dizzy and afraid. His fingers strained to count the things he knew. The world was a shining bomb.

LAW

She stood on the steps of the Capitol Building, raising and lowering her foot in an exaggerated way, vicious scowl on her lips.

What am I doing? she said.

Got me, I answered.

She rolled her eyes. She turned instead to look at a mother breastfeeding her baby on a nearby step. The mother smiled at her.

See you, she said.

At the bottom of the stairs, she sprinted across a dirt lot and into the doors of the arboretum, there lost among the vines and flowers and gross abundance.

In an hour, my phone rang.

Hey, I said.

There was the sound of whinnying or monkeys. Capitol punishment, she answered.

WORK

She put a potato chip at the edge of the rug and the dog, tired, got to its paws and behind its nose. The dog went back beneath the table—potato chip, then again.

She watched him tap into the computer. Fuck, dude, she said.

His eyes not there, behind the glasses.

Fuck, dude, she said.

He closed the computer.

She got up from the rug with the sunlight slicing her legs in its pretty way. There was more sun here day by day than anywhere. One day, sun, and two. Three.

She stood by him. He touched her thigh. She stood there, and he patted her.

Fuck, dude, she said. They laughed.

The dog looked up, tail in its graceful curve.

Basho : Champ of Haiku : Comes for Late Summertime Lunch

Annie is eleven and she reads the newspaper religiously. On the way home from nightshift, Mom stops in at the 7-11. Annie prefers paper to online, though she's sorry a bit every day for the trees.

As it's summer, Annie takes the paper out back, under the oak. There is the little iron table and the heavy iron chair. Dad is passed, the pond he made is filling with silt, yet there's still water enough for the lotus—its flowers float cosmically pink.

Annie reads the news. The president battles Congress. The lost celebrity is found broken in the hills. Unemployment rises or falls. Congress battles the president.

As it's summer, Annie has next to nothing to do. Late lunch with Mom before Mom goes to bed. Wander the yard with bare legs and feet. Miss Dad with his pink and soft hands. Talk to the neighbor's black and white cat. Ask him why he always wears a tuxedo.

After the news, Annie visits her friend. Sandra is seven. She doesn't much care for the news but she's especially nice. You can play with any of these, says Sandra, sweeping her hand over her collection of trucks.

What to know about Sandra is that she wets the bed. Annie discovers this only today. Sandra, Sandra's mom says, is much younger than you. Annie excuses herself in a rush.

Annie sits under the oak. The crows crow-crow at each other. Mom is inside preparing late lunch. Annie is scared—she's much younger than you. How the little green frog, ka-plash! hits the pond.

The quiet pond
A frog leaps in,
The sound of the water
—Matsuo Basho

BIRDS

She was typing her dissertation, something about animal consciousness, when he came in holding a lawn chair.

Where'd you get that? she said.

He set it in the center of the room. It fell from a tree. Or maybe the sky. It's warm.

She bent forward, holding the laptop close to her belly so it wouldn't slide to the floor. *Kinda* warm.

It was warmer before. He put one finger, a little pink and a little brown, to the chair's back, which was a little bit pink and a little bit brown.

Which tree? And what do you mean? The laptop fan was whirring.

Look, he said. All I know is I heard it hit the ground. I turned around and there it was: lawn chair.

Hmm, she said. I suppose that's pretty weird.

Yeah, he said. I suppose it is.

She went back to her dissertation. He stood by the slowly cooling chair and watched her type.

WATCHING PAINT DRY

It's a warm Saturday night. My front door is open. I hear the people on their way past my house. The young men tell jokes. The young women laugh musically. There is alcohol on their voices.

I go to Amazon. I look through the free movie selections on my account. I read the reviews: Mesmerizing; The acting is terrible; One of the best movies I've seen; Like watching paint dry.

I pick the one with the one-star reviews.

I watch the movie. Two men sit in a bar and talk. A woman and a man walk down the street holding hands.

I pause the movie. I get up from the couch and go to the front porch. I light my cigarette.

A man and woman walk by my house. The young woman makes a joke. The young man laughs musically. They take each other's hand.

I go back to my movie. There is trouble. The two men have an argument. The two lovers break up.

I pause the movie again. I go out to my porch. An older man walks by. He's smoking a cigarette. A young woman walks by. She's leading her dog on its leash.

I finish the movie. The last scene in a hotel room fades to black.

I lay on the couch. I hear people walk by my house. They laugh musically or they are alone.

I fall asleep. I dream of a long and waveless lake.

Barbie Football

We sat on the metal steps behind Belinda's house and smoked hollow twigs. We used a whole box of matches because they kept going out and probably gave us cancer. A blue jay stilt-walked through the grass on ridiculous purple legs.

Two days, said Belinda, and it's off to God Fucker school. Belinda said they loved God so much down there they wanted to fuck him, every day.

Why go? I answered. Though I knew. Her best friend from church—Anne—was already there and wrote Belinda how awesome it was. How all the kids would watch hillbillies ride through campus on their moonshine donkeys. I doubted Anne called it God Fucker though. She wore pink barrettes that said PTL.

You can come too, Belinda said, waiting for me to give her one in the shoulder. She knew I hated God more than she did.

Nah, I said, not taking the bait. It's off to Shitzville Middle for me. We lived in the north, snow as normal as anything, and Belinda's new school was in Kentucky. It scared me, thinking of dark mountains, kudzu, weird children and their pigs.

So, I asked. One more game?

She shook her head. I don't do that anymore.

So you say.

So I know. She stretched out her legs, the dirty red jeans she always wore, put her hand on her crotch. God wants me to save it for my husband.

I never got how serious she was being. Not even in second grade when she said to put my hand in her underwear. I did, she let me keep it there like 10 seconds, then ran off laughing, shouting that a naughty boy had molested her.

C'mon, I said. One more. You know they aren't going to let you play down there. Though I wondered, would they? They might play Truth or Dare at Christian school. If they let Belinda go there, they'd let anyone.

Never again, she said. She kissed her palm—a thing she'd just started doing—and pressed it up against the sky. She said, Stop being so horny anyhow. I see your pants.

I rolled my eyes. Stop looking then.

No, she said. Stop bulging then.

You like it, I said.

She stuck out her tongue, screwed her eyeballs around in a ridiculous way. What if I do? Is it a G-D crime?

I got up from the steps, went into the yard. I kicked the deflated Barbie football into the bushes. I don't want to see you again, I said at her, over my shoulder. I just don't want ever to see you. I went to the bushes, got to my knees. I was sorry about the Barbie football. I couldn't see, wiping my eyes. I can't find it, I said. It's not even here.

THE ARTIST (A FICTION)

A boy collected stones from his driveway in the rain. The stones were orange, green, silver, and blue. He liked the worn stones the best, smoothed and rounded over with time, but at times those that flaked, sat fragile in his hand, attracted his drifting eye.

He took his bucket of stones inside, up the stairs, to his bedroom. He lay them out on his dresser top and then, for the moment, forgot about them.

The next day, his mother, an artist, said to him, What a wonderful exhibit!

Thanks, Mom, the boy said, remembering the stones, elated.

He went to his room. There they were, his exhibit, laid out on his dresser top.

Shit, he said. The once colorful set of stones, now dry, were more or less gray, brown, beige. The tender oranges, the forest greens, reduced to dull powder.

Mom, he said, pride reduced to embarrassment, These suck. The bucket of stones hung loosely in his hand. They're ugly, he said, and boring.

His mother, a mother, hugged her son. I'm sorry, she said.

The boy took his bucket outside. He cast the stones into his driveway, a broadcast of disappointment. The stones lay where they fell, forgotten for now, a length of quiet years.

THE RETURN

The bottle is blue, plastic, a red cap, filled with a medicated powder. When it is empty and thrown away, it rides nearly to the dump, bouncing out of the truck's hopper and into the culvert. A heavy rain pushes it a half mile to the tidal creek. When the tide comes in, then out again, the bottle bobs along, past stands of reeds, a sweep of ducks, and into the bay.

The man is in his small boat, lifting his pots by their lengths of rope. In each pot a crab or two waves its claws, blue and bright in the faintly falling rain. Mostly they are too small, or female, or the man feels sorry for them, and he drops them over the side to sink elegantly back to their murky bottom. Most times the boat sputters home with few to no catches at all.

The man in his boat spies the bottle amidst a float of bay grass loosened from its roots. He guides the boat close, reaches out with his net, brings the bottle aboard. Into the hull it goes, alongside pieces of Styrofoam buoys—sun and salt faded—a potato chip bag, a half-empty bottle of red Mountain Dew.

Before 9 the rain clears and the sun comes out, biting and white. The man, without his hat today, steers the boat towards home. It's a quarter mile across the open water, chopping at the keel. The wind freshens, dries the sweat across his arms, from the sockets of his eyes. At the small wooden dock of home, he is home.

The pieces of buoy, the potato chip bag, the plastic bottles go into the trash. This makes the man feel strong, less than his 75 years. He has done good unto the world. He has done well. At the rear door to his home he turns back to look at the bay, loudly blue under the sky. He has done well. He is hungry. His ailing wife is asleep in their bed, her breath catching, quitting, starting again.

She said, Look how god put that spiderweb at the corner of the window, just so. The falling sun struck its threads with chalk, gray, a wisp of pink.

I think, he said, we could thank the spider for that.

She smirked. The spider, god, the devil, me, Kevin Bacon, the dog... The dog, realizing she'd been referred to, thumped her tail twice somewhere in the other room ... What's the difference? What's the distance?

He shrugged. There's at least two of those I don't believe in.

She opened the refrigerator, the light button sticking for a moment, popping out then, doing its work. Okay, she said, look how *you* put the spiderweb at the corner of the window.

He took her glass of iced tea, held it to his forehead. Phew, he said, this heat—I *wish* I didn't exist.

She nodded. Now you got it. Now you're onto it. That's the stuff.

He took a sip of tea, handed it back to her. In fact, I have no idea what you're talking about. No idea what anyone's talking about. He made as if to grope the air around him.

I can see that, she said—smiling. She ran the tap, jiggled, shook the spent bottle of hand soap. This is out, she said. All out. Out!

The dog appeared in the doorway then, believing it was time for a walk.

How to Write Flash Fiction

Begin

Begin with a thing. Make it a sparrow. A sparrow clinging to the stem of an Easter Lily. Make the sparrow silent. We don't want too many voices this early on. Let the lily speak for itself.

Enter

Now, enter. This is how things get going. You need a dog. This dog is red but the top of its head is blonde, bleached by the sun. The dog swims every day. Get that dog moving! Don't forget about the sparrow. The blonde dog looks at the sparrow.

Tension

Your palms should sweat! But not too much, remember this is flash fiction. The bird is small, remember that. It is frightened of the dog and might leave the lily, remember that. How are your palms? How's it going?

Complication

You don't have time for this. Why does this dog swim so much? It's an Easter Lily, but in July? Get out of this place as fast as you can.

Plot

By now you should have thought of this. An old man wants something. Between him and that: a silent sparrow. How will he get that? I don't even think the dog is his, so that won't help. Oh, this is getting good.

More

This is where there is more. I don't know what to tell you. More please.

Climax

You should look at all these creatures. How much competition for the heart! The old man has a stained shirt and has almost got something. The blonde dog is barely an inch from the sparrow. The tiny feet pierce the lily's delicate skin.

Space

Give us a second to catch our breath. We are tired, and full.

End

I've taught you well, haven't I? Flowers and animals, the sky, how it all will fall. You're falling—now. Put your last period. You've done everything you could.

Setting in Flash Fiction

There is a summertime forest. It's been a wet year and the moss on the trees is a florid green. In the bright day, each tree leaf is a cupped-hand of shade, blue-black against the sun-blue sky. Green, black, and blue.

In the distance a stream bubbles. It is the idiom of things that were once here: Rusted Model A deep in the muck, stone-piled walls, buried ash under fallen chimneys, door-yard of periwinkles.

It smells like stone. It smells like things that cannot, will not, move. That and a distant threat of rain.

The tall grass on the clearing is blades, of course, black mat of brown needles beneath the tree. And the hidden insects, worms about the roots, black beetles in the scruff. The grass is soft—knives—soft again, the tiny cuts as the wind shifts.

Then, with the storm, the pressure of the birds, the bowed fiddleheads. The stream is in disarray.

The fawns in the underbrush shout for their mothers.

Character in Flash Fiction

Don Stella Herb Guinevere Thanh Warren Jesus Omar
Fred Mahamadou Josephine Maria Arjun

Robin Nuthatch Starling Jay Chickadee

Spot Champ Princess Ellie Rover Goodboy Cocoa Mellie
Rob

You Me Them Her Us

Rock River Sky Glen

Industrialist Waitstaff Driver King Phlebotomist
Underemployed Dentist

Elbow Heart Enamel Toe Humerus Hackles Tongue

Pyramid Church Hut Mall

Hack Rube Dipshit Aleck Greenhorn Mark Narc
Cheapskate Pig Goat Get

Snake Wolf Vampire Sabretooth Bear

Universe Multiverse Verse

Twelve Fifty Pi Thousand Zero Googol Half

Lily Oak Ivy Moss Kudzu Mayapple Wort Alfalfa Carrot
Duckweed Aloe Peyote Milkweed

Saint Bodhisattva Angel Beloved Sweetie Seraph

Sign French Pidgin Swahili Khmer FORTRAN Secret
Latin Academic

Death Life Bardo Walmart

Perspective in Flash Fiction

A woman looks out her window: On a hillside dowsed in flowers a man plays cat's cradle. He plays for hours and in endless configurations: x and *X* and x. He will not eat or drink, though he will wipe his brow and mark the place where the sun sits in the sky: ⎯ or ⎯ or —

The woman looks out her window: Her daughter sits in the garden surrounded by gardenias. The child smells a flower and smiles: :). She smells another flower, which might be the same flower but from a different glance, and smiles: ;)

The girl and the man are daughter and father, or father and daughter, depending on where you stand. To the woman at the window they are despair or love, depending on where she sits.

A woman sees outside her window: A child or a man. Turned in a daughter's string, a father's smile, they can't know which is which: ox xo

Time in Flash Fiction

Start with a woman drinking whisky. Have her drink for an hour. Darling, she'll slur, marry me. Live for me always.

She is a little girl. Her dog has been lost somewhere in a field. That field is a thousand acres of yellow flowers, each a sun that sets on the seconds that the little girl cries. Darling! she shouts—the name of her dog.

The woman has a baby and she is drunk. The baby can't stop crying. She thinks, This baby is my life forever! She hates the sun that will never stop falling on her baby's face.

She is an old woman, about to die. Her daughter stands beside her hospital bed. The daughter's legs ache and she wants to go home. Her mother whispers, Please remember me always.

End with a teen and her can of Sprite. Have her sip for a second. Her legs are sleek and long, hirsute with a golden fuzz. Baby! she'll bark—the older boy who never leaves her alone.

Joseph Young lives in Baltimore, MD, where he writes, sometimes makes art, and looks at things. His book of microfictions, *Easter Rabbit*, was released by Publishing Genius in 2009. He self-published the novel, *NAME*, dubbed vampire realism, in 2010. In 2018, he created MicroFiction RowHouse, a project for which he installed text throughout his home—on the walls, windows, ceilings, and many other surfaces—to tell the story of a fictional family who might have once lived in the home. In 2019, he self-published *Always Never Speaking: 50 Flash Fictions, with commentaries by the author.*

ACKNOWLEDGMENTS

The stories "Something About Easter, Maybe," "A Pair of Men," and "Orientation" appeared in *Frigg Magazine*. "How to Write Flash Fiction" appeared in *New World Writing*. "Fauna of My Front Yard" appeared in *Urban Creatures Blog*. "A Spanish Acre" was arranged and recorded by Boat Water for their EP, *A Boat Water Christmas* (2022). "Barbie Football" appeared in *Atticus Review* and "Basho" in *Wigleaf*. "The Thing I Was Trying to Tell You" appeared in *The Art of Everyone*.